WANTED

Nature/Nurture

A Story on Adoption

Written and Illustrated by

Susan Calder-Heaps

AF231411

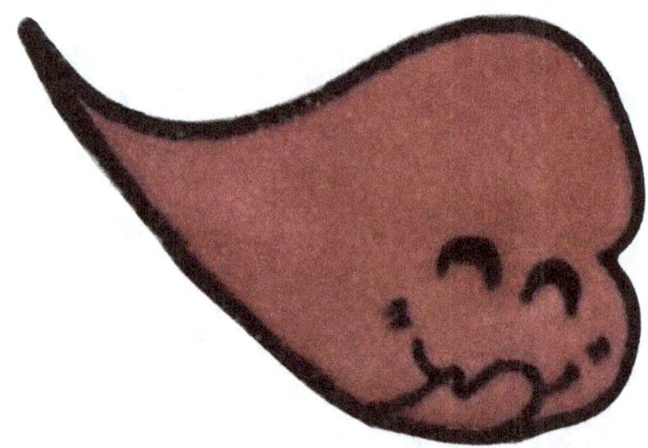

Copyright © 2026 Susan Calder-Heaps

All rights reserved. No part of this book may be reproduced, stored in a retrieval system, or transmitted in any form or by any means, electronic, mechanical, photocopying, recording, or otherwise, without prior written permission from the author, except for brief quotations in critical reviews or articles.

The scanning, uploading, and distribution of this book via the Internet or any other means without the permission of the author is illegal and punishable by law. Please purchase only authorized editions and support the author's work.

ISBNs:

E-book: 978-1-970894-53-0

Paperback: 978-1-970894-54-7

Hardcover: 978-1-970894-55-4

LCCN (Library of Congress Control Number): 2026902855

This book is dedicated

To my fantastic family

and for the love of families ...

PROLOGUE

When people, who are thinking of adoption,

hear that my children have come into my life in different ways,

they almost always ask,

"Is it the same?"

It is most definitely the same!

When you carry a baby in your 'tummy' (your womb) for nine months

or wait long months on an adoption list,

you imagine what your baby will look like;

yet when they place your baby in your arms for the first time ...

he/she does not look at all like you imagined ...

but you have already fallen in love!!!

Chapter 1: SUPERBOND!

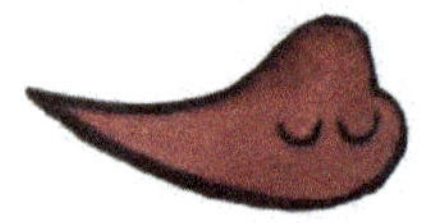

Here's a wonderful thought!

... a family decides that they would like to adopt a little baby . . .

The mother loves children, and after they have been to Family Services and registered their desire for a baby,

the process starts . . .

Eeeeks!!!Exciting!!!

The mother, let's call her **Maggie,**

already has three darling little girls and

because she came from a family of *six* kids,

more children would be wonderful in completing her nest.

Maggie enjoys every day,

watching her three little girls grow and develop.

As she watches her little ones at play,

her heart swells with pride and love for her children!

Then she starts to think about the new little baby

who will soon join them...

and now

her heart starts to *swell with love* for the new baby boy.

She hasn't even seen him yet!

What will he look like?

Will he have brown hair or blond hair?

Will he have blue eyes? Green eyes? Or brown eyes?

She can hardly wait!

<u>It reminds her</u>

of when she carried her other babies in her tummy (her womb);

she couldn't see them or know what they looked like

but she knew that she loved them soooo much

and they continue to grow in her heart!

The new baby

started to grow in Maggie's heart, too. . .

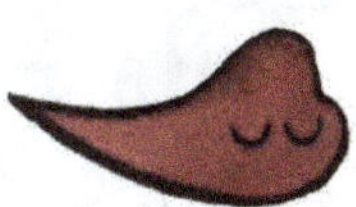

The day came! The <u>call</u> came!

"Your baby is here. Be in Bransen at 3:00 p.m. on Friday."

Oh, my goodness!

It was really happening!

Maggie's new baby had finally arrived! The girls' new brother is here!

They were exciting days!

Were they ready? Did they have enough diapers?

Two more days to wait ...

it seemed like forever after waiting two years!

The trip to Bransen was long!

The parallels to going into natural labour and delivery,

were uncanny.

They went into an anti-room,

a similar emotional experience to a labour room.

They signed papers

and waited anxiously ...

Then they heard a baby cry in the next room

and they knew ...

That was their baby!

It reminded Maggie

of the first time that she had heard her other babies' cry;

it was before she got to see them or hold them

for the first time.

A social worker brought him in

and placed him in Maggie's arms.

As she held her little six-week-old baby for the first time,

he engaged her.

The more she talked to him,

the more he cooed back.

He slipped into their hearts!

Maggie fell in love all over again,

just as she did when she first saw each of her girls for the first time!

"Is it love that brings you here? ... or love that brings you life?" (Paul Stookey)

When the girls met their new brother,

they were filled with love, too!

He cooed and spit bubbles on them!

Everyone laughed!

They had been talking and thinking about him

for a very long time!

It was a looooong wait ...

There is a bond of love with children,

That grows in a mother's heart!

Nobody can describe it!

You have to experience it.

It is rich and it is perfect!

It is super incredible!

It's a superbond!

SUPERBOND!

Superbond!

That incredible glue that sticks things together!

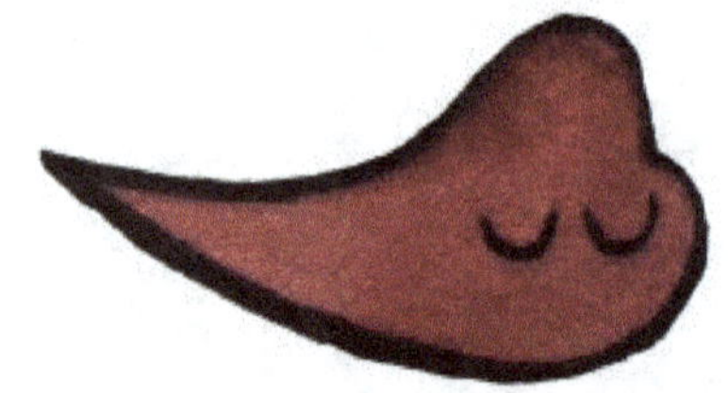

If you glue two pieces of paper together,

once the glue is set ... you cannot separate them!

They are stuck together like skin on our body!

Like skin on our body,

if any of it is removed by a scrape or a cut,

it hurts!

Our skin stays on us forever!

It is SUPERBONDED!

Adoption is a little bit like that.

A child is bonded to his/her family!

Like the graft on a tree ...

A child is bonded to his/her Mother and Father, brother and/or sister!

There are grandparents, aunts, uncles, and cousins!

It's a SUPERBOND!

That is how God beautifully puts families together!

For our young readers,

SUPERBOND

is our superhero!!!

He is shaped like a heart, and he represents LOVE!

Swishing through the air,

he spreads love wherever he goes ...

Now,

that makes a **GREAT** superhero!!!

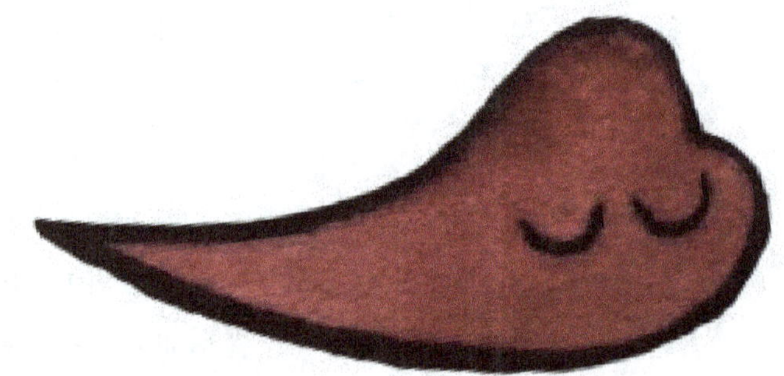

Let's take a look at the Family Tree together ...

Chapter 2: THE ROOTS

A tree is fed from the roots up.

The roots of a tree

give it stability,

feed it,

helping to make it

strong and stable …

The roots of our family tree,

are the people who have gone before us,

have influence those who have raised us,

make us who we are today. (nature/nurture)

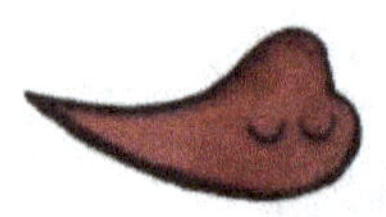

These thoughts and influences from a granddaughter to her grandmother are an example of how just one person, now an ancestor for others, has had an impact on all of us! The roots of a family tree are of huge importance, as those roots continue to feed the tree! We are who we are because of the influence of love, values, empathy, etc... that filters up into our parents and other family members. This is how we live and develop into successful members of society. We are who our roots are...

A – a name that took me days to learn & gave me much to brag about

N – never without stories to tell

T – the greatest supporter of all her kids (grandchildren alike)

O – over a hundred rhymes passed on by my mom, i.e. ...

I – "it is better to burp and bear the shame than squelch the belch and suffer the pain"

N – never complains

E - extra bags of Halloween goodies to assure leftovers

T – the glue that bonds a large family together

T - the packages of small sugared cereal boxes for the morning after a sleepover

E – excellent mother, grandmother, and woman

More Thoughts on the positive influence just one person can have in our family tree...

... Exciting, dedicated, incredibly witty, thoughtful, hostess with the 'mostess',

 cheesy Ritz crackers, eating at Grannie's creation ... the Pig Table, crossword puzzles,

 interested and interesting, lavender scented objects, Irish eyes that smile

a very hip grandmother ... right down to the Birkenstocks, Oreo cookies, cranberry juice

object of much admiration, never a mess when she trimmed your bangs, the masking tape caught it all! Nobody would dare make a face in Grannie's photos ☺,

Easter egg hunt with plastic mugs bearing the owner's picture, lunches with Grannie and Grandad ... yummy! many hours of much-appreciated woodwork staining ☺,

undoubtedly the best gift giver, roast beef and Yorkshire pudding,

proudly displays the artwork made by her grandchildren's hands, having friends in every city I went to ... who Grannie said, "would love to see me", yummy Sunday dinners,

sweet peas, cool, Abby and Ann Landers articles used to convey a moral lesson ☺,

teaching me how to make aluminum trays (thank you), little rosy cheeks ... especially after "giddy juice", incredible chef, family, the spelling of her surname, "double f as in funny face"

Influencers/Roots

With whom our parents and family members (aunts, uncles, cousins, etc …)

share values …

"More Memories of Maggie's Influencers"

When Maggie thinks back to the three generations who have influence her ... the influencers: she thinks of a grandmother who was one of the first lady doctors and a suffragette, she thinks of the line of doctors and nurses, the pioneers, the very holy people who walked with God, those who had struggles but pushed through them, the positive attitudes, the workers, the givers, the servants of a generation ...

Chapter 3: The Graft

(Nature/Nurture)

As this tree grows,

a graft is added.

"Is it love that brings you here,

or love that brings you life …"

(Paul Stookey)

As the graft takes hold.

It is also fed from the roots of the tree.

(The Power of Three Generations,

especially!)

<u>The graft cannot grow and thrive without

the root system!</u>

Nature and nurture take over!

Within no time, the graft becomes one

with the tree!

It cannot be separated.

There's a superbond!

The ancestors' "blood line" feeds the graft

along with the rest of the tree.

The "blood line" of their values, their love, their history

and now ...

It is no longer a graft,

but one with the tree.

No longer a graft,

but one with the tree.

You now have the 'blood line 'of the tree,

The ancestors

And all connected to it!

It's yours! ...

These are your roots! Your influencers.

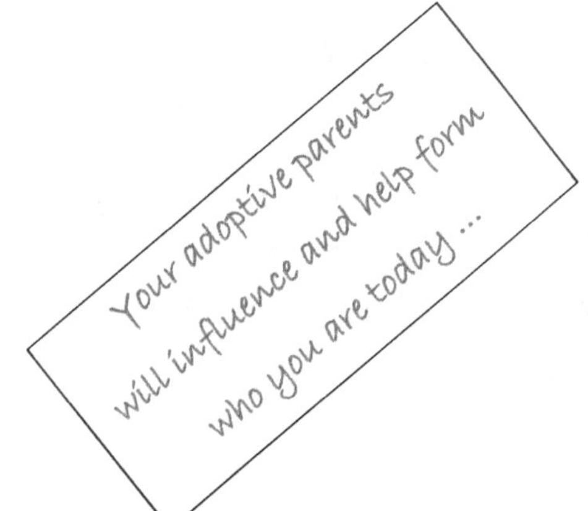

"The Power of Three Generations: before and after you …

In order to find out who you are and what you want,

start connecting with yourself

and understand your belief system.

Your mom and dad, grandparents, and great-grandparents

have so much information that can help you find patterns.

Keep the positive ones and change the things that make you feel stuck.

That means

what you do today also impacts the 3 generations after you. This is where you can find your

purpose.

Believe in yourself and trust your intuition."

Again, remember …

"What you do today

also impacts

the 3 generations after you.

This

is where you can find your purpose.

Believe in yourself

and trust your intuition."

(Forest of Mothers Coaching, printed with permission)

"... like a mighty oak, how deep your roots go ...
and I will love you fiercely and watch you grow ...
Know that though you may travel and roam
Your roots will always bring you back home."

(Excerpt, printed with permission from **ROOTS...**
a book written and illustrated by Chelsea Warren of Victoria, BC)

Postscript

In our uncle's home,

there is a chair made from wood that was grown

... a mistletoe attached to another tree,

possibly an apple tree.

The colour of the grains

is very different in this example,

but it shows you how two trees

have become one beautiful piece of wood!

Today,

the chair is about 175 years old.

We're so happy that our ancestors kept these treasures.

<u>Author's Note:</u>

It is important

to acknowledge here that there are people

with whom we have never met . . .

who have given their child to us

so that he/she can have

a better upbringing than what they were able to offer at the time.

Because Maggie is a mother and knows a mother's love,

she thinks about another mother,

who would always wonder about her little boy

and if he is okay . . .

and Maggie made a commitment a long time ago,

to think about her

and send her mental messages, often . . .

"He is doing well and he is loved . . .

Thank you for the wonderful gift!"

www.ingramcontent.com/pod-product-compliance
Lightning Source LLC
Chambersburg PA
CBHW080507030726
47592CB00011B/3284